TIMBUCTO NEIG...

A sort of horse from Timbuctoo

a story by
Roger Hargreaves

© Mrs Roger Hargreaves 1999
Published in Great Britain by Egmont World Ltd.,
Deanway Technology Centre, Wilmslow Road, Handforth,
Cheshire, SK9 3FB.
Printed in Italy
ISBN PBK 0 7498 4350 0
ISBN HBK 0 7498 4420 5

NEIGH was a sort of horse.
A Timbuctoo Horse.

He lived in a field,
on the island of Timbuctoo.

And he didn't like it!

You see, every time it rained,
his furniture got wet!

"I really must find somewhere else
to live," he thought, "but where?"

He went for a walk to think.

He met **WOOF**.
Woof was a sort of dog.

"Hello," he said to Woof. "I'm trying
to think of somewhere to live!
Where do dogs live?"

"In dog kennels," said Woof.

"What a good idea," said **NEIGH**.

And went back to his field, and built himself a horse kennel!

It was very uncomfortable!

"I don't like living in
a kennel," thought **NEIGH**.

And went for another walk
to think where to live.

He met a worm.

"Hello," he said to the worm. "I'm
trying to think of somewhere to live.
Where do worms live?"

"In worm holes," said the worm.

"What a good idea," said **NEIGH**.

And went back to his field
and dug himself a horse hole!

It was very, very uncomfortable!

"I don't like living in a hole," thought **NEIGH**.

And went for another walk to think where to live.

He met **QUACK**.
Quack was a sort of duck.

"Hello," he said to Quack.

"Hello," said Quack.

"I'm trying to think of somewhere
to live," said **NEIGH**.

"Oh," said Quack.

"Where do ducks live?" asked **NEIGH**.

"On a duck pond," said Quack.

"What a good idea," said **NEIGH**.

And went back to his field, and
made himself a horse pond!

It was very, very, very uncomfortable.

And rather wet!

"I don't like living in a pond,"
thought **NEIGH**.

That evening, as he sat in
his armchair in the middle of his field,
NEIGH felt very miserable.

"I don't like living in a **FIELD**," he thought.
"But I like living in a **KENNEL** even less
than a field.

And a **HOLE** even less than a kennel.

And a **POND** even less than a hole.

Oh dear!"

And he went to bed.
In the middle of the field.

The following day he went for yet another walk to try and think yet again where to live.

"There must be somewhere better than a field," he thought.

And do you know something?

CLIP-CLOP, CLIP-CLOP!

He met somebody who gave him
a very good idea of where to live.

"What a good idea," he said, and went
back to his field to build it.

And he lived happily ever after.

CLEVER NEIGHHHHHHH!

In his **HORSE NEST**!

MMMMMMM, COSYYY